ALIS  THE AVIATOR

WRITTEN BY

DANIELLE METCALFE-CHENAIL

PICTURES BY

KALPNA PATEL

tundra

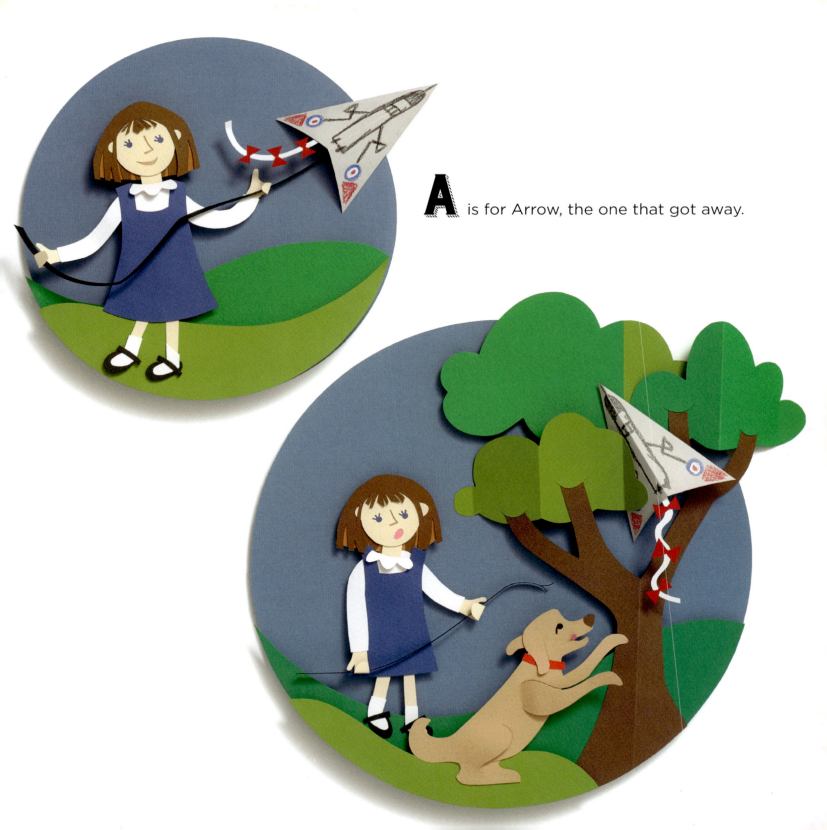

A is for Arrow, the one that got away.

B is for Beaver, great for work and play.

C is for Chipmunk,
a small and nimble plane.

YUKON TRANSPORTATION MUSEUM

CF-CPY

Canadian Pacific

D is for Dakota, a northern weather vane.

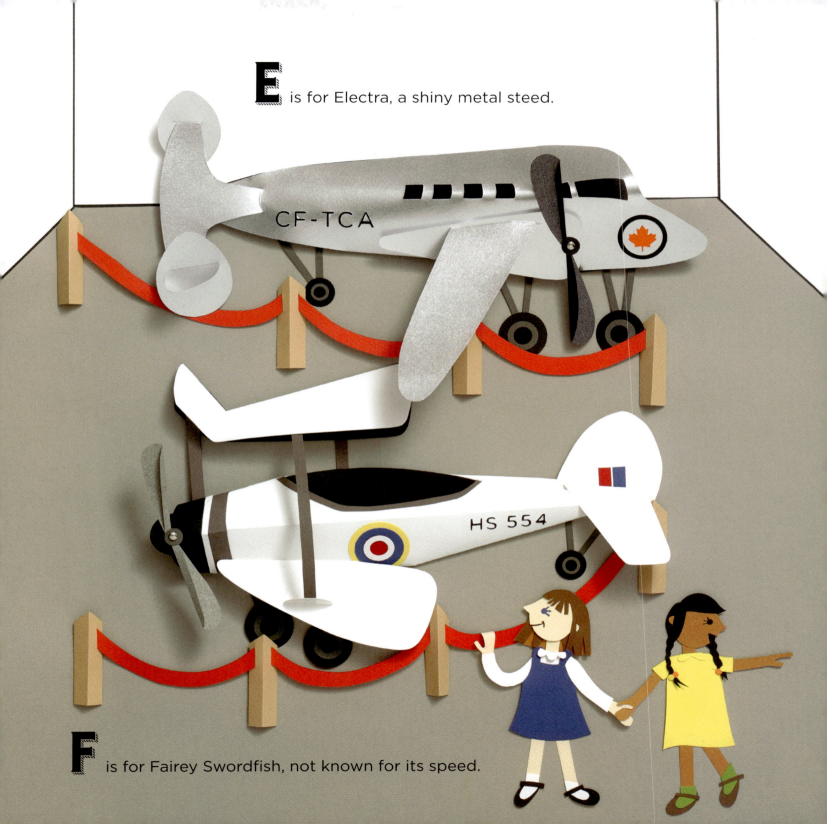

E is for Electra, a shiny metal steed.

CF-TCA

HS 554

F is for Fairey Swordfish, not known for its speed.

G is for Goose,
a swanky flying boat.

H is for hot air balloon, up above it floats.

I is for Islander, a well-known island hopper.

J is for Jet Ranger, a useful type of chopper.

K is for King Air,

the best twin turboprop.

L is for Lancaster, known for wartime drops.

RY

F

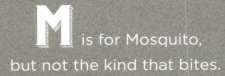
M is for Mosquito,
but not the kind that bites.

N is for Norseman, but not the kind that fights.

CF-SAN

O is for Otter,
the Beaver's bigger brother.

P is for parachute, a jump like no other.

HEROIC HOUNDS

Parachute Dog Awarded Medal

Parapups Save the Day!

Q is for Queen, which crashed into the loam.

☆ **The Whitehorse Star** ☆

TWENTY EIGHTH YEAR   WHITEHORSE, YUKON, MAY 11, 1928

Queen of the Yukon Badly Damaged

G-CAHR

QUEEN OF THE YUKON

. . . a plane you build at home.

S is for Silver Dart, the first in Canada's skies.

C-FCIX

1214

T
is for
Tiger Moth,
a pilot's first try.

U is for ultralight, a bird's best bud.

V is for Vampire,
sucks gas instead of blood.

W is for Waco,
two wings instead of one.

X is for experimental — not quite done!

Y is for York, a transport to the North.

Z is for Zeppelin, explorers setting forth!

DR. ALIS KENNEDY

The Alis in this book was inspired by a real pilot: Dr. Alis Kennedy. Alis has spent her life helping people and animals, going on adventures and pushing the limits.

She's been a lifeguard and a scuba diver, had a summer job as a flight attendant with Air Canada and had her paintings displayed in galleries. She is fluent in French and English, and she also speaks Spanish and Michif — a Métis language. In fact, Alis is related to Louis Riel, the famous Métis political leader.

Alis joined the military at age 18 and served for more than a decade with the Navy Reserve, where she had top secret security clearance. She also served in the Royal Canadian Air Force (RCAF) for a short time.

"I flew in a T-33 Silver Star when I was in the military," she says. "The pilot let me fly, and I did some maneuvers all by myself! In those days, women were not allowed to fly military aircraft — and I actually wasn't even a pilot then. But that experience (and flying a DC-3 for four hours before) made me want to fly on my own."

It was after this that Alis got her private and commercial pilot's licenses — likely the first Indigenous woman in Canada to do so.

Alis has many university degrees, but she's not a medical doctor — she has a doctorate in psychology, and she was a probation and parole officer for 22 years. She *did* help deliver a baby in the remote rainforest though, and she rescued young people from drowning at sea. She's even been to South Africa to help save cheetahs!

Today, this pilot, veteran and founding leader of the Warriors and Veterans Society (Council of the First Métis People of Canada) lives near Toronto. There, she volunteers with eleven different organizations, and was a proud flagbearer for the Invictus Games in 2017 for wounded, injured and sick Servicemen and women.

Alis has received many awards, but the one that means the most to her is the eagle feather. The eagle is a symbol of strength, courage, wisdom, honesty, power and freedom; an eagle feather acknowledges a person's hard work and achievements. It is one of the highest honors that can be awarded to Indigenous people.

GLOSSARY

BEAVER: the DHC-2 Beaver is a hardy and versatile bush plane introduced in 1947 by de Havilland Canada. There are stories of Beavers hauling everything from sled dog teams in the North to pianos during the Vietnam War. Dr. Alis Kennedy got to fly in one when she was volunteering along the Amazon River in Peru!

ARROW: the Avro CF-105 Arrow was supposed to be the fastest interceptor jet in the world when Canadian engineers began building it during the Cold War, but the project was scrapped in 1959.

CHIPMUNK: the DHC-1 Chipmunk was built just after WWII as a single-engine trainer for new military pilots in Canada and the United Kingdom. "Chippies" are known for being great for aerobatics, and you can still occasionally see pilots performing tricks in them.

DAKOTA: the Dakota has a few names — Douglas DC-3, C-47 Skytrain — depending on whether it was used for military or civilian use. Flown by airlines and air forces since the 1930s, there are still some flying regularly today. One plane, CF-CPY, is on a pedestal in Whitehorse, Yukon, and actually turns with the wind, making it the world's biggest weather vane! Dr. Alis Kennedy got to fly one when she was in the military at C.F.B. Shearwater.

ELECTRA: the Lockheed Electra was an American all-metal plane built in the 1930s, when passenger airlines were first getting started. Famous pilot Amelia Earhart flew a modified Electra on her around-the-world expedition in 1937 — the trip where she mysteriously disappeared, never to be seen again.

FAIREY SWORDFISH: this biplane torpedo bomber was flown by the Allies off of carrier ships during WWII. The "Stringbag" became famous because it flew so slowly the German ships couldn't shoot it down.

GOOSE: the Grumman G-21 Goose was an amphibious airplane first used to fly businessmen to and from work in the Long Island, New York, area. That's not a bad commute!

HOT AIR BALLOON: nowadays we usually think of festivals and sightseeing trips, but hot air balloons in the past were used by armies to see what their enemies were up to and by explorers in the Arctic.

ISLANDER: the Britten-Norman Islander is used on the shortest scheduled airline flight in the world: the trip from Westray to Papa Westray in the Orkney Islands, Scotland. It only lasts one minute!

KING AIR: the Beechcraft King Air is a twin-turboprop aircraft first made in the 1960s — but it's still considered the best in its class.

LANCASTER: Lancasters were huge four-engine bomber aircraft used by the Allies during WWII. Most of the early ones were built in England, but in 1942, they started manufacturing them at Victory Aircraft in Malton, Ontario, where a quarter of the employees were women.

JET RANGER: Bell Jet Rangers have been used since the 1960s by the American Army as well as by lots of commercial and private operators. They've also been used to set around-the-world helicopter flight records, with the pilots landing on ships to refuel.

MOSQUITO: the de Havilland DH.98 Mosquito was a versatile two-engine, two-crew aircraft the Allies flew during WWII. The Mosquito was made almost entirely out of wood, which earned it the nickname Wooden Wonder, but many simply call them Mossies.

NORSEMAN: the Noorduyn Norseman was a popular Canadian bush plane in the 1930s, but there are still a few flying around the world today. Each summer, people gather in Red Lake, Ontario — the Norseman capital of the world — for a festival to celebrate this rugged plane.

OTTER: the DHC-3 Otter was made by de Havilland Canada after the early success of its "little brother," the Beaver. It's known as a short takeoff and landing (or STOL) aircraft, because it doesn't need much space to start and stop.

PARACHUTE: parachutes are essential aviation gear — and not only in case of emergencies! Thrill-seekers, paratroopers and fire-fighting "smoke jumpers" use them, and, during WWII there were even "parapups": trained dogs that jumped out of planes alongside rescue workers.

QUEEN: the *Queen of the Yukon* was a Ryan B-1 monoplane, sister ship to the *Spirit of St. Louis* flown by Charles Lindbergh on the first solo non-stop transatlantic flight in 1927. Unfortunately, the Queen crashed in 1928 in Whitehorse, Yukon, and was beyond repair.

RENEGADE: the Murphy Renegade is an open-cockpit biplane you can build yourself at home from a kit. It weighs about 400 pounds (181 kilograms), though, and definitely requires skill and the right tools (and probably an extra-big garage)!

SILVER DART: Douglas McCurdy, a young engineer, and the famous Alexander Graham Bell executed the first powered aircraft flight in the British Empire on February 23, 1909, in Baddeck, Nova Scotia. *The Silver Dart* flew 870 yards (800 meters) before McCurdy set her down gently on the ice.

TIGER MOTH: the best-known training airplane ever, this open-cockpit biplane lets instructors sit in back with a student up front. Over 8,000 were built by the end of WWII, and they were flown by many air forces, from Australia to South Africa to Brazil.

ULTRALIGHT: many pilots say ultralights are the closest they've ever come to being a bird, and in fact, some have used ultralights to help train geese to migrate from Ontario to Virginia. Dr. Alis Kennedy got to fly in one over the breathtaking Victoria Falls in Zambia: "What a view I had!"

VAMPIRE: this distinctive frontline fighter jet started out doing various air force operations — including the Winter Experimental Establishment in Edmonton, Alberta. In 1949, the Blue Devils Vampires became the Royal Canadian Air Force's aerobatic team, performing at 45 air shows until they were disbanded in 1951.

WACO: these sporty little vintage biplanes can still be spotted with either closed or open cockpits doing sightseeing tours and performing in air shows.

EXPERIMENTAL: new aircraft types (or modifications to existing ones) take a lot of research, development and testing. Until they're approved as safe for use, they're called experimental — sometimes you'll even see an X along with their registration number painted on the airplane.

YORK: the Avro York was developed by the British during WWII for airlifting troops and cargo. After the war, it hauled equipment and supplies to the North when Canada and the United States worked together to create the Distant Early Warning (DEW) Line.

ZEPPELIN: the most famous of these historic German-made airships are the Graf Zeppelin and the Hindenburg, which made transatlantic flights and, in the case of the Graf, did a famous polar flight. Some now think modern-day blimps could be used in the Arctic to airlift cargo into remote places and as military airships.

For Andre: I can't wait to see where your wings take you — DMC

To Mom and Dad — KP

Text copyright © 2019 by Danielle Metcalfe-Chenail
Illustrations copyright © 2019 by Kalpna Patel

Tundra Books, an imprint of Penguin Random House Canada Young Readers, a Penguin Random House Company

Library and Archives Canada Cataloguing in Publication
Metcalfe-Chenail, Danielle, author
Alis the aviator / Danielle Metcalfe-Chenail ; Kalpna Patel, illustrator.
Issued in print and electronic formats.

ISBN 978-1-101-91905-7 (hardcover).—ISBN 978-1-101-91906-4 (EPUB)

1. Alphabet books—Juvenile literature. 2. English language—
Alphabet—Juvenile literature. 3. Aeronautics—Juvenile literature.
4. Women air pilots—Juvenile literature. I. Patel, Kalpna, illustrator
II. Title.
PE1155.M547 2018   j421'.1   C2017-905568-2
                                               C2017-905569-0

Published simultaneously in the United States of America by Tundra Books of Northern New York, an imprint of Penguin Random House Canada Young Readers, a Penguin Random House Company

Library of Congress Control Number: 2017951212

Edited by Samantha Swenson
Designed by Kelly Hill
The artwork in this book was rendered in cut paper.
The text was set in Gotham and Burford.

Printed and bound in China

www.penguinrandomhouse.ca

1 2 3 4 5   23 22 21 20 19

Penguin
Random House
tundra | TUNDRA BOOKS